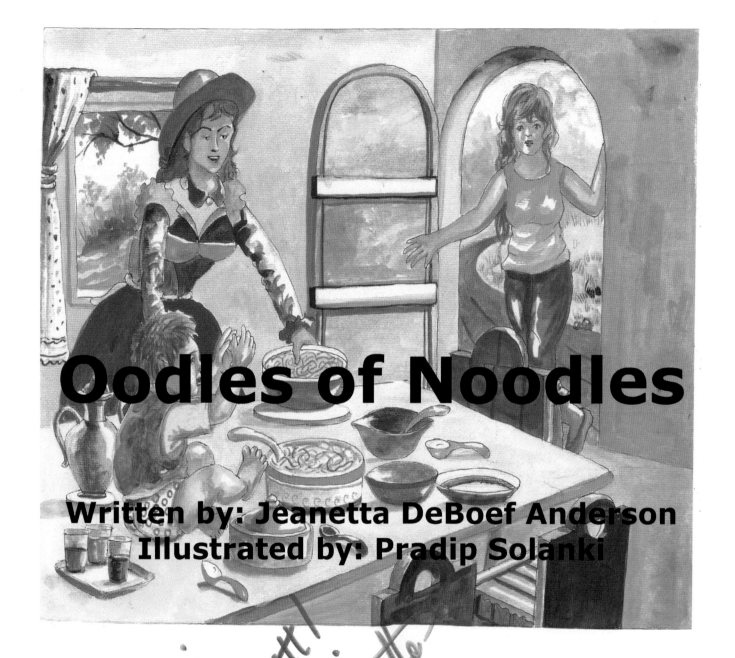

Oodles of Noodles

Written by: Jeanetta DeBoef Anderson
Illustrated by: Pradip Solanki

For: Garrett
Jeanetta

Dedicated to

Grandma DeBoef

who was great at making the most

of every situation – good or bad.

"Spaghetti for supper again!"
grumbled Lizzie as she sat down to dinner.
"Gettie, gettie," squealed her little brother
as he clapped his chubby hands together.
Lizzie rolled her eyes at him as she thought
about how simple life is when you're little.

Dad had been around a lot more lately,
and mom had said that money was going
to be a bit tight these days.
And now, three to four times a week
there was some form of pasta on the dinner table.
I mean, come on, **she thought to herself,**
I know times are hard,
but can't we be just a little bit more creative than this!
She mindlessly shoved spaghetti into her mouth
feeling quite sorry for herself.

Later, after helping clean up the kitchen,
Lizzie did her homework and headed off to bed.
That night, as she slept, dozens of pasta characters
danced through her dreams!

Mama Manicotti sat

On her ravioli tuft to doodle

While sister Campanelle chased

Fusilli their noodle poodle.

Next, Papa Bowtie puttered up

In his lasagna buggy

And ran to greet his family

With a great big squishy huggy.

He spotted baby Tortellini

Giggling gleefully

While squishing meatballs that had fallen

From their spaghetti tree.

Then Uncle Elbow skidded up

In his cavatelli wheels

And pastamania broke loose

As everyone danced and squealed.

Out back, Grandpa Corkscrew

Relaxed on his rigatoni stool

While Grandma Corkscrew splashed

In their huge anelli pool.

Just then, Mama Manicotti

Said that it was time for grub

So they all grabbed a ravioli tuft

And sat around a great big tub.

The tub was filled with rice

Of every kind and size

And Lizzie stared in amazement

(she couldn't believe her eyes)...

She watched them fill their little shell bowls

Clear up to the brim

Then reach into their pockets

And with a silly noodle grin,

They each pulled out a vial

Of their very favorite hue

And dripped three little droplets

Into their ricey stew.

Then took their ziti chopsticks

And stuffed their sticky faces

Until their tummies were so round

They could not tie their laces!

Then they happily licked

Their little round lips

And waddled out the door

Swinging their ricey hips.

Rice was all they ate

(with an occasional egg roll)

Yet they always seemed thankful

For what was in their bowl.

Lizzie awoke with a grin.

"*What a strangely amusing dream that was,*"

she exclaimed aloud!

As she began getting ready for school

she thought about her dream.

All through the day she couldn't get

that silly dream out of her head.

The more she thought about it,

the sillier she grinned!

It had been a long time since she had been

so amused about something.

Suddenly, a light bulb popped on in her head.

Perhaps, **she thought,** *Being happy and content*

isn't about what you have or don't have.

Perhaps it's about making the most

of every situation – good or bad!

A few days later, as she sat down
with her family to their pasta dinner,
Lizzie felt that silly grin
creeping at the corners of her mouth.
She heaped her plate full of pasta
and then reached into her pocket.
This pasta, **she said to herself,**
is going to be the best pasta
I have ever tasted.

And it was!

Vocabulary Words:

Amazement – a feeling of being very surprised

Amusing – funny or enjoyable

Chopsticks – a pair of thin sticks used to pick up and eat food

Content – satisfied; not needing more

Creeping – moving very slowly

Doodle – to draw something without thinking about it

Gleeful – full of happiness or satisfaction

Grub – a slang word referring to food

Grumble – to complain about something

Hue – a color or shade of a color

Mindless – paying very little attention or thought to

Pastamania – crazy celebration done only by pasta people

Putter – to move slowly

Tuft – a footstool or low seat; cushion

Vial – very small container

Waddle – take short steps moving from side to side like a duck

Discussion Questions:

Why did Lizzie think that life is simpler when you are little?

Why do you think Lizzie's dad had been home more?

Why were they eating pasta so often?

What is another word for pasta?

Who is your favorite pasta character?

What were the pasta people putting into their rice?

Why do you think they were doing that?

What lesson did Lizzie learn from the pasta people?

What did Lizzie do the next time she ate pasta that reminded her to be thankful?

What are some ideas of how to make the most of every situation – good or bad?

Noodle Knowledge

Manicotti

Fusilli

Ravioli

Bowtie

Campanelli

Lasagna

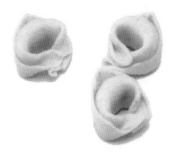

Tortellini

Corkscrew

Elbow

Rigatoni

Cavatelli

Anelli

Shell

Ziti

Other Titles by Author:

Ma Pumpernickle's Pumpkin Patch

Upcoming Titles by Author:

December Frost

Made in the USA
Charleston, SC
14 October 2016